To James and Sophie, with love
— L. T.

For my mother, Frances Bronson,
with all my love
— L. B.

Henry Holt and Company, Inc., *Publishers since 1866*
115 West 18th Street, New York, New York 10011

Henry Holt is a registered trademark of Henry Holt and Company, Inc.

Text copyright © 1998 by Lindsey Tate / Illustrations copyright © 1998 by Linda Bronson
All rights reserved.
Published in Canada by Fitzhenry & Whiteside Ltd., 195 Allstate Parkway, Markham, Ontario L3R 4T8.

Library of Congress Cataloging-in-Publication Data
Tate, Lindsey. Teatime with Emma Buttersnap / Lindsey Tate; illustrated by Linda Bronson.
Summary: An informative look at the history of tea and tea parties presented in the form of a story.
Includes recipes. 1. Afternoon teas—Juvenile literature. 2. Tea—Juvenile literature.
[1. Afternoon teas. 2. Tea. 3. Parties.]
I. Bronson Linda, ill. II. Title. TX736.T38 1998 641.5'3—dc21 97-40697

ISBN 0-8050-5476-6 / First Edition—1998 Typography by Meredith Baldwin
Printed in the United States of America on acid-free paper. ∞
1 3 5 7 9 10 8 6 4 2
The artist used acrylic and oil paints on board to create the illustrations for this book.

Teatime with EMMA BUTTERSNAP

Lindsey Tate illustrated by *Linda Bronson*

Henry Holt and Company *New York*

Hello! My name is Emma Buttersnap and I want to tell you all about tea and tea parties. My Great-Aunt Prudence is an expert on tea, and we have tea parties whenever we can. You can, too. Try saying "Great-Aunt Prudence" a couple of times and you will find that it is quite a mouthful. That's why I call her Aunt Pru instead.

Aunt Pru lives in England with her cats, Lapsang Souchong and Jasmine. They are named after two types of tea. I visit at least once a year, and we always have a special tea party. We sip our tea with our pinkies out and pretend we are eating with the Queen of England.

This year I am invited to a birthday tea, but Aunt Pru won't tell me whose birthday it is.

"My lips are sealed," she says.

Last year I learned that not all tea parties are social occasions.
The Boston Tea Party was one of the events that led to the American
Revolution. When Aunt Pru came to visit, we went to the Boston Tea
Party Ship and Museum.

*In the eighteenth century, the British government put a high tax
on tea, making it very expensive. American colonists grew angry because
they did not want to pay more money to the British, so they decided
to do something about it. On December 16, 1773, two ships packed with tea
arrived in Boston Harbor from England. That night a group of men crept
on board the ship and dumped 342 chests of tea into the sea in protest.
Their actions became known as the Boston Tea Party.*

Aunt Pru and I climbed aboard the *Beaver II*, a full-size replica of
one of the ships that the colonists boarded. We threw a crate of tea
over the side of the ship and then hauled it back in. In this way we
pretended to protest without polluting the water in the harbor.

What I especially like about a tea party is that preparing for it is as much fun as throwing it. First you must decide who you are going to invite. You could ask just one person, maybe a few friends, or your entire class (but get permission first).

I ask Aunt Pru again about our birthday guest.

"It's a surprise party for a very special person," she says. She is better at keeping a secret than I am.

I do know that my mom and daddy and our friend Mr. Leaf are invited to the celebration. That makes five of us—not including our guest.

Suddenly I have a thought. I know who the birthday guest might be. "We're going to have tea with the queen!" I shout, as I run off to practice my curtsy.

Invitations

A written invitation is the best way to let your guests know about the tea party. Aunt Pru sends out cards with pictures of Jasmine and Lapsang Souchong on them, but I like to create my own teapot invitations. You can make them, too.

To make teapot invitations you will need:

- Construction paper
- Magic Markers or crayons
- Teapot stencil
- Scissors

You could draw flowers on your invitations for a spring tea or teddy bears for a teddy bear's picnic tea. Whatever you choose, just remember to include all the important information: the date, day, and time of the tea party, and your address and telephone number. Don't forget to let people know if the tea party is for a special occasion or if it has a theme.

Teapot Stencil

"Why do tea parties usually start at four o'clock?" I ask Aunt Pru as she comes into the kitchen.

"It's a tradition," she says. "The story goes that an English lady, the Duchess of Bedford, experienced 'a sinking feeling' in the late afternoon between lunch and dinner, rather like the hungry feeling you get when you come home from school. So she started to invite a few friends over for tea and toast. Then cakes and sandwiches were added. That is why tea parties now happen between lunch and dinner."

"But we've had tea parties at breakfast," I say.

"That's true, but that's because we like them so much. It's okay to bend the rules a little now and again, Emma."

Over the centuries, tea has saved millions of lives because it forced people to boil their drinking water, and this helped to kill germs and prevent terrible diseases like cholera.

the Menu

Once you've decided upon the guest list and sent out the invitations, then you will need to think up the menu. Usually teas consist of small sandwiches, scones (special types of biscuits), and little cakes. Sometimes Aunt Pru and I stick to familiar tea party food, and sometimes we don't. We've come up with lots of variations to our tea menus because it's so much fun.

Today we are making cucumber sandwiches, peanut butter and banana sandwiches (my favorite), scones with jam and cream, and a chocolate birthday cake. And of course there will be a large pot of tea.

Once we have done all our shopping for our food ingredients, Aunt Pru and I go off to buy the tea. We are lucky because there is a shop nearby that sells just tea. The owner of the shop is our friend Mr. Leaf.

Inside it smells warm and spicy. The tiny shop is filled with every type of tea you can imagine. There are three thousand different kinds of tea, and it seems as if Mr. Leaf has them all. Tea bags and tea leaves, herb teas, fruit teas, and flower teas. Teas from all over the world—China, India, Japan, Sri Lanka—with names like Russian Caravan, Chingwoo, Lapsang Souchong (like Aunt Pru's cat), and Tippy Golden Flowery Orange Pekoe. Mr. Leaf uses special words when he describes teas to customers—smoky, delicate, bitter, red liquor, fine aroma—and they just roll off his tongue. "All the way from India," he'll say sometimes to a customer, or "From the other side of the world" as he points to a country on his globe.

The Origins of Tea

Mr. Leaf knows everything there is to know about tea. The first thing I wanted to know when I met him was where tea comes from. This is what he told me:

"Tea leaves begin life on a bush called *Camellia sinensis*, a type of evergreen tree that can grow to thirty feet in the wild. But in tea plantations the shrubs are cut back to three feet because it is much easier to pick the leaves at this height."

"Do machines pick the leaves?" I asked.

"No, all picking is done by hand, usually by women. A good tea picker can pick forty pounds of tea a day."

"That's enough for a lot of tea parties," I said.

"The pickers use their thumbnails to nip two leaves and a bud from the tea plant. Originally the Chinese used monkeys to pick tea leaves!

"Here's where it gets complicated, Emma. After picking, the leaves are spread on trays to dry out. Next, they are rolled and sieved by machines. Rolling releases each leaf's oils, and sieving separates the big leaves from the smaller ones. Then the tea is fermented. This means that the leaves are exposed to warm, damp air. They change in color from green to brown."

"But what about green tea?" Green tea is one of Aunt Pru's favorite teas. "Does that come from a different plant?"

"Good question, Emma," said Mr. Leaf.

"There are three types of tea: green, oolong, and black. Almost all of the tea drunk in England—and in America—is black tea. All the teas come from the same plant and are processed in the same way until fermentation. Green tea is not fermented at all, and oolong tea is fermented only for a short while, and that is the difference."

"How does the tea get to us?" I wanted to know next.

"When it is ready for shipping it is packed into large wooden tea chests and transported to seaports, where it is stored in the holds (or bottoms) of ships. Each chest can carry about one hundred pounds of tea."

In the early days of tea, the journey from China to America by sea could take from six to twelve months, and often the tea would be moldy on its arrival. Faster ships were built. These clipper ships were lean and sleek with lots of sail. By 1845 a clipper ship could travel from China in 102 days, and an all-time record of 74 days—less than three months—was soon reached. Clipper racing from China to London started, and the first tea to arrive on the London market brought the best price.

Today we are buying some Earl Grey tea from Mr. Leaf. This is a blend of Chinese and Indian teas mixed with oil of bergamot. A bergamot is a small, pear-shaped orange. It makes the tea smell fresh and lemony. We buy some tea with caffeine and some without—decaffeinated. My parents prefer that I drink decaffeinated tea. Sometimes I even drink herb and fruit teas (or infusions as they are also called) because they don't have caffeine in them.

"Is this for today's party?" asks Mr. Leaf. "I'd better give you my finest then. Only the best for our birthday guest," he adds and smiles.

"See you at four o'clock," I call out as we leave.

Tea contains a substance called caffeine, a natural chemical stimulant. In decaffeinated drinks the caffeine has been taken out. Some people feel caffeine gives them energy, while others argue that it keeps them awake all night!

Making the Tea

No tea party is complete without a pot of tea. Aunt Pru has taught me how to make a perfect pot. Here's how you do it.

Please remember to ask an adult for help since boiling water needs careful attention.

⑤ Fill a kettle with cold water and bring it to a boil.

⑤ Pour a little of the boiled water into a teapot. Swirl it around the pot once or twice and then pour it out. This is to warm the teapot.

G Add one tea bag or one teaspoon of tea per person to the teapot, up to the maximum number of cups of water that your teapot can hold.

G Pour the boiled water into the teapot. Put the teapot lid on, and if you have a tea cozy (a special cloth cover) then slip it onto the teapot. Wait five minutes for the tea to brew and then pour it into cups.

Did you know that tea bags were invented by a tea merchant who sent out samples of his tea in small silk bags? He got dozens of requests. Nowadays filter paper is used instead of silk, and the smallest tea leaves are put into the bags.

Tea can be drunk plain or you can add milk. Some people like to add sugar or honey. I like lots of milk in my tea. Milk with just a drop of tea is called cambric tea—it's delicious and Aunt Pru says it's a good way to start tea-drinking. My mom always has cambric tea. If you enjoy lemon in your tea, don't also add milk because it will curdle and taste terrible.

Tea has been popular in America since about 1670 but it has been in existence for more than four thousand years. It was first drunk in China, and then it was introduced to Japan and India. It only made its way to Europe and America when explorers from the West reached the tea-drinking countries at the beginning of the seventeenth century.

Aunt Pru told me two stories about the origins of tea. One version is that Shen Neng, a Chinese emperor, was having some drinking water boiled when a few leaves from an overhead bush fell in and scented his drink. He liked the taste so much that he spread the word about this wonderful new drink. The other story involves an Indian monk who fell asleep during meditation. To punish himself he sliced off his eyelids and buried them in the earth. A tea bush grew from the "seeds" the next day. I think I like the first story better!

Aunt Pru and I start our tea party preparations with a relaxing cup of tea. It has become a tradition.

"What a wonderful cup of tea," says Aunt Pru, as she sips her cup of Earl Grey.

Teapots

For your tea party a teapot is the only special equipment you will need. A simple ceramic pot will do the job, but teapots come in all shapes and sizes. Aunt Pru has a special teapot collection. She buys teapots at flea markets and antique shops—anywhere she can. Some of them have quite a history.

Her most valuable teapot is a Yixing teapot from nineteenth-century China. The Chinese started making these pots in the 1500s. Yixing teapots were made from a special kind of clay, and no two are known to be alike.

Aunt Pru's cauliflower teapot is also rare. It was made by Josiah Wedgwood in England in 1765. Aunt Pru said most of the teapots he created were classical in design, but he made one teapot collection in the form of fruits and vegetables: pineapples, cabbages, and, of course, cauliflowers.

Aunt Pru never uses these two teapots. She keeps them on display in a china cabinet. Her other teapots are all quite usable.

"Let's use the cat teapot today," she suggests.

In about the fourteenth century the Chinese
began to brew tea leaves just like we do today,
and to do so they invented the teapot.

Tea Sets

Whole tea sets were created around teapots with matching milk jugs, sugar bowls, cups, and saucers. It's nice to have a tea set, even though Aunt Pru and I often use pretty cups and saucers that don't match.

When tea was popular in the eighteenth century, ladies used to carry their own teacups to parties in special cases. About one hundred years ago, mustache cups were widely used in England. These cups have a ledge running around the inside on which the drinker rests his mustache so that it will stay dry.

Preparing the Finger Treats

Before you start to prepare the food for your tea party, always remember these safety tips:

- Wash your hands before and after handling food.
- Check with an adult before cooking.
- Ask an adult for help or supervision when using sharp knives or scissors, and when using the oven.
- Wear an apron to protect your clothes.
- Wear oven gloves when handling hot dishes.

For our tea parties, Aunt Pru and I usually figure that our guests will each eat two whole sandwiches (that equals about six or eight sandwich pieces). Tea sandwiches are delicate and easy to eat. They are made with thin bread and the crusts are trimmed before they are cut into pieces. You can cut your sandwiches into squares, triangles, hearts, or any shape you like.

The sandwich is named after the Earl of Sandwich, who once called for some food that he could eat with his hands while playing a game of cards. He was served some meat between two hunks of bread.

Recipes

Peanut Butter and Banana Sandwiches

8 thin slices bread	4 tablespoons peanut butter
Butter	1 ripe banana

Lightly butter each slice of bread. Spread 4 tablespoons of peanut butter onto 4 slices of bread. Cut the banana into thin slices and lay the slices on top of the peanut butter, dividing the banana evenly. Top the banana with the remaining slices of buttered bread. Trim the crusts. Cut each sandwich into 3 or 4 pieces. Yield: 12 to 16 tea sandwiches

Cucumber Sandwiches

8 thin slices bread	1 cucumber
Butter	Salt and pepper to taste

Lightly butter each slice of bread. Peel the cucumber, and carefully cut it into paper-thin slices. Place the cucumber slices on 4 slices of bread and season with salt and pepper. Cover with the remaining 4 slices of bread. Trim the crusts. Cut each sandwich into 3 or 4 pieces. Cucumber sandwiches are very refreshing. It is important that the cucumber is sliced very thin.
Yield: 12 to 16 tea sandwiches

Scones

1 cup flour	1/2 stick butter
2 teaspoons baking powder	2 tablespoons light cream
1 tablespoon powdered sugar	Milk and sugar for glazing

Preheat the oven to 400 degrees. Mix the flour, baking powder, and sugar in a bowl. Add the butter in little pieces and rub it in with your fingers until the mixture looks like crumbs. Add cream and mix until a light, soft dough forms. Scatter a little flour onto a work surface and roll out the dough with a rolling pin until it is 1/2 inch thick. With a round 2 1/2-inch cookie cutter, cut out 8 circles (you may have to gather the dough together and roll it out again to do this). Brush the circles with milk, sprinkle with sugar, and place on a buttered baking sheet. Bake in the oven for 10 to 15 minutes. Serve warm, and eat with butter, jam, and cream. There is much argument on the correct pronunciation of the word "scone." Some rhyme it with "on" while others rhyme it with "bone." Take your pick. Either is acceptable! Yield: 8 scones

Chocolate Cake

1 heaping tablespoon cocoa powder   3/4 cup sugar

2 tablespoons hot water   3/4 stick butter

1 cup self-rising flour   2 eggs

1 teaspoon baking powder

For chocolate icing:

2 ounces semisweet chocolate, broken into pieces   1/4 stick butter

Preheat the oven to 350 degrees. Grease an 8-inch cake tin. Blend together the cocoa powder and hot water in a small bowl. Mix to a smooth paste. In a large bowl mix together the flour, baking powder, sugar, butter, and eggs. Spoon in the cocoa powder paste, then stir the ingredients with a wooden spoon. Mix thoroughly to make a soft cake mixture. Spoon the mixture into the cake tin and spread until level. Place in the center of the oven and bake for about 30 minutes.

    To make the icing, fill a small saucepan halfway with water and bring to a simmer. Remove pan from heat. Set a small mixing bowl containing the broken chocolate pieces and butter over the saucepan. Stir until the chocolate has melted and the ingredients are blended. Pour the chocolate icing all at once onto the top of the cake. Spread over the top and around the side of the cake using a knife. Let it stand for at least 45 minutes before eating.   Yield: 8 servings

Here are some other food ideas for your tea parties:

Egg and Cress Sandwiches   Gingerbread Men

Honey Sandwiches   Pita Bread Pizzas

Grilled Cheese Sandwiches   Brownies

Cinnamon Toast   Banana Bread

Cupcakes   Gingerbread

Pancakes   Sticky Buns

Shortbread

Setting the Table

My favorite part of the tea party preparation is getting the table ready for the guests. First I cover the tea table with a cloth. Then I write out the menu on a small piece of paper. The menu can be decorated with stars, glitter, stickers, or whatever you like. Name cards are another nice touch so everyone knows where to sit. You can make these by folding small pieces of paper in half. (Try to spell everyone's name correctly!) I set the surprise birthday guest in the best chair at the end of the table. Fit for a queen, I think.

Place mats are fun to make, too. Aunt Pru taught me how to make doilies—paper mats that look like lace.

To make doilies you will need:

 Several sheets of paper (white or colored)

 Scissors

Remember to ask an adult for help when you use scissors.

Fold the paper in half, in half again, and in half a third time. Cut small shapes (squares, triangles, or semicircles) along each edge. Once you have finished, fold the rectangle in half one more time and cut a square in the center of each new fold. Then open the paper. You have just created a beautiful doily.

Aunt Pru says that flowers brighten any table. If you can, pick a small bouquet of wildflowers for the center. Or maybe you have a flowering houseplant. Aunt Pru has a nice idea for today's tea party. She has brought in a small branch of leaves. They are red and gold, and will look pretty as a centerpiece.

Each guest needs a plate, a cup, and a saucer. Serve the sandwiches and cakes on large plates or serving platters. Remember to put plates of food at each end of the table so there won't be too much stretching to do. Assemble the teapot, milk, and sugar on a tray in the kitchen, and when the guests arrive, boil the water for the first pot of tea. Don't forget to provide knives for cutting scones, small forks for eating cake, and spoons for serving jam and cream.

Throwing the Tea Party

Aunt Pru and I are all ready for our guests. The table is set, the food is on the table, and the teapot is waiting in the kitchen. The food smells delicious. I am tempted to take a sandwich but Aunt Pru insists that would be impolite.

"Do you have candles for the cake?" I ask suddenly.

Aunt Pru smiles. "Yes, lots of them."

The doorbell rings and it is Mr. Leaf. "Come in," we say, "and sit down." A cold wind swirls in behind him.

"What you need is a good cup of tea," says Aunt Pru.

The doorbell rings again and I wonder if the surprise guest has arrived. Instead it is my mom and daddy. They have been out in the country all day and their noses are red with cold.

"Happy Birthday!" they yell.

"Happy Birthday!" bellows Mr. Leaf.

What do you know! The surprise birthday guest is Aunt Pru! She truly *can* keep a secret.

"Happy Birthday!" I shout, as I show Aunt Pru to the seat of honor at the end of the table.

"Sorry I'm not the Queen of England," she says with a chuckle. Soon the house is filled with warmth and laughter. The kettle is boiling.

It is time to eat.

Aunt Pru and I are always very excited at our tea parties but we never forget our teatime manners. As the hosts, it is up to us to make sure that everyone has enough to eat, and that the teacups are always filled. People often worry about the do's and don'ts of teatime—should they add milk or tea to their cup first? Should they spread their scone with jam first or cream? Aunt Pru and I say don't worry. Drink up and enjoy yourself!

When the sandwiches and cake are finished it's time to read our fortunes. Mr. Leaf is first. Aunt Pru takes Mr. Leaf's cup. She swirls it around, studies his tea leaves, and warns, "Beware of black cats." At that moment Jasmine leaps onto the table for some cream. We all giggle and Mr. Leaf seems relieved that Jasmine is a striped cat.
    Then Aunt Pru squints into my cup and puts on her huskiest voice. "My goodness, my dear, what do we have here? A crown and a scepter. It looks like you have royalty in your future, Emma."
    I gaze into my teacup and peer at the scattered tea leaves. When I look up, the Queen of England is sitting at the end of the table.
    "Welcome," I say. "Would you like a cup of tea, Your Majesty?"
    At last I can try out my curtsy.